The Adventures of Paddington™

Hatching Chicks

HarperCollins *Children's Books*

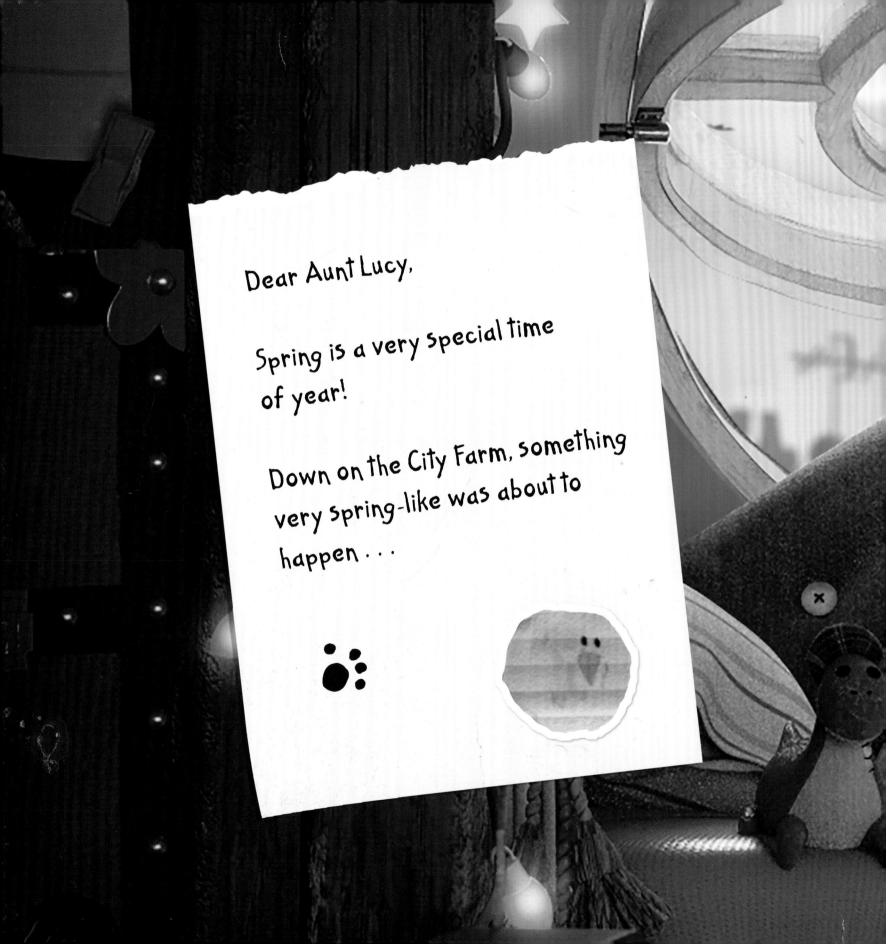

Dear Aunt Lucy,

Spring is a very special time of year!

Down on the City Farm, something very spring-like was about to happen . . .

Paddington was at the City Farm with Jonathan, Judy and Simi. They were gazing at **three eggs,** waiting for something amazing to happen.

"I wonder where Orla, the mother hen, is?" whispered Paddington.

"Orla's at the vet," said Baaz, the owner of the farm. "Could you look after **her eggs** while I collect her? They are going to hatch into chicks very soon."

"You can **count on us**, Baaz!" said Paddington.

Baaz put a lamp over the eggs to keep them warm and then left for the vets.

"We could each choose one egg to look after," suggested Judy. Jonathan picked the biggest egg. Judy picked one with markings on the shell. Which left Paddington with the pale egg.

"Now all we have to do is wait for them to hatch . . ." said Jonathan.

CRRRRRAAAAACK!

"Ohhh!" they gasped in surprise as Jonathan's egg suddenly cracked open.

A tiny fluffy chick peeked out of its shell and hopped over to Jonathan.

CHEEP! CHEEP!

"Welcome to the world," Paddington said softly.

"I'll look after you," said Jonathan, cradling the chick.

CRRRRRAAAACK!

"Oh, here comes *my* chick!" gasped Judy as her egg cracked open.

A second fluffy little chick peeked out, but instead of going to Judy it hopped over to Jonathan.

"Hey, I'm over here!" cried Judy.

"This little chick loves me too," said Jonathan, carefully holding one in each hand.

"Ahhh," sighed Paddington. "So cute!"

"Hmm," said Judy. She wasn't so sure.

CHEEP! CHEEP!

"I'm not going anywhere until you hatch," whispered Paddington to his egg.

Luckily, he had an **emergency marmalade sandwich** under his hat.
But as he didn't know how *long* he'd have to wait, he decided to eat it
v e r y   s l o w l y.

"Maybe I can help?" said Simi, handing him a folded chair to sit on.

Suddenly Gertrude ran away, bleating loudly.

MEEEHHHH!

"Oh no!" cried Simi, dashing after her. "Gertrude! Come back!"

Paddington tried to pull one end of the chair down. It pinged back!

He opened one side, then the other . . . *ping!* Both sides sprang shut!

"Oh, bother!" he said.

Finally, he opened both sides and quickly sat down. He was about to take a bite of his sandwich when suddenly . . .

PING!

. . . the chair snapped shut on him like a clamshell, knocking his sandwich clean out of his paws!

"Woah!" cried Paddington.

After Simi freed Paddington from the chair, the young cub went to check on his egg.

The bulb on the lamp suddenly fizzed out. "Oh dear," said Paddington. "There must be some way for me to keep my egg warm . . ."

Paddington was just about to sit on the egg when Simi spotted him. **"Paddington!"** cried Simi. "You might **squash** it!"

PFFFT!

Simi suggested putting **Aunt Lucy's woollen hat** on the egg instead.

"That's better!" said Paddington.

CHEEP!

On the other side of the farm, Jonathan was having lots of fun playing with the chicks. Judy wanted to join in . . . but the chicks kept running straight past her!

The chicks followed Jonathan everywhere!

"The three of us are like one big happy family," said Jonathan.
Judy felt left out. She wished she could find a way to make the chicks like her too.

Shortly after, Judy had an idea. She made a costume, painted her face and started pretending to be a hen!

"CLUCK, CLUCK, CLUCK!

I'm Mummy Hen," said Judy, flapping her wings. The chicks backed away.

"Er . . . I think you're scaring them," said Jonathan. "You're scaring me too!"

"I'm sorry," sighed Judy. "I'm just jealous that the chicks like you more than me."

"Maybe you're just trying too hard?" suggested Jonathan.

Judy crouched down and the chicks hopped on to her wing. She couldn't believe it!

Meanwhile, all the waiting for the egg to hatch had made Paddington feel **very sleepy.**

"Must . . . stay . . . awake . . . ahhhh," he yawned.

Simi found Paddington upside down in a bucket!

"Are you okay, Paddington?" she asked.

"Not really," he replied. "But I need to be **uncomfortable** so I stay awa . . ." He started to doze off and fell . . .

SPLAT!

. . . in a wheelbarrow full of food scraps.

"Ohhh!"

But it was no use. Paddington soon fell
fast asleep. When he woke up, he had a
big surprise . . .

"Oh no!" he gasped. "It's hatched!"
But where was the chick?

Just then, Baaz came back with Orla, the mother hen.

"Are you okay, Paddington?" he asked.

"I don't know where the little chick has gone," said Paddington, feeling upset.

"Don't worry!" said Simi, lifting the shell to reveal a tiny tortoise underneath. "Look!"

Paddington was confused. "The chick has turned into . . . a baby tortoise?"

"I must have **mixed up** the hen's egg with the tortoise's egg,"
explained Baaz. "What a silly sausage I am! I think I might know
where the chick is . . ."

The **third chick** was with the **mother tortoise!** It saw the mother hen and hopped over to her and the other chicks, just as the baby tortoise scuttled to *its* mother.

"Ahhh," everyone sighed happily.

The little ones were back with their mothers
and it was more than worth waiting for, Aunt Lucy.
Spring is such a wonderful time of year!

Love from,
Paddington